MW01644980

STRAIGHT 2 HELL

NOVELLA BY WANDA JONES

Contents

FIRST DAY OF SCHOOL

On an early Monday morning, Bean Mother walked into his room blissfully to wake him and his sister up. She politely says, Wake up, it's time for school. Bean looks with a disgusting stare on his face as if his mother said something that was unhumanitarian and replies. School? (Bean's mom replies.) Yes! School. And ask Bean, in a confusing tone, Is there a problem son? Bean rises up out of the bed looks sad and speaks. Yes, I don't have anything to wear. Bean's Mother looks with an unease look and speaks. Son! What do you mean you don't have anything to wear? What happened to your pants from last year, they were still good? Bean looks up at his mother and replies. This is the first day of school and all the other kids will be wearing new clothes and shoes except for me. Bean Mother giggles and speaks. And you really believe that son, that every kid except for you will be going back to school with new clothes and shoes. Bean looks and replies. Yes, all the ones I know. Bean mother looks optimistic and speaks. I doubt that very seriously son, and anyway. I don't send you to school to show off new clothes and shoes I send you to get an education.

Bean looks disappointed and speaks under his breath. How can I focus on getting an education, when I'm too worried about having clothes on my ass. Bean Mother looks in a shocking manner and asks. What did you say Son? Bean looks and replies. Nothing ma'am. Bean's mother then replies. Look, I'm doing the best that I can, and I know you want new clothes like your friends, but I don't have it, but when I get the money, I promise I'll buy you a new pair of pants, so please be patient and do what I ask of you, son. Bean then looks sorrowful, apologizes, and speaks. I'm sorry mom, I know you are, but! Bean stepdad abrasive interrupts and replies. But my ass, little punk, who do you think you are? Like you go to work and pay some damn bills around here? Bean mother becomes terrified and tries to intervene by saying. Todd, he didn't mean anything by it. Todd suddenly grabs Bean mom by the throat and asks. Who the fuck is talking to you, Bitch! don't interrupt me when I'm talking, that's the problem with his ass now, always trying to save his little soft ass. Bean stands there and stares at his stepdad in an anger manner. Bean stepdad then asks. Little punk, you have something to say, I'm right here, say it to my face. Bean continues to stare his stepdad down as if words could kill. Bean mother then responds frantically and says Son, take you and your sister and go finish getting ready for school. Bean looks at his mom as if he didn't want to leave her and then she yells. Now! Bean slowly walks away and grabs his sister Tai by the hand and leads her out the room as if he were protecting her. Soon as the door closes Bean's mom apologizes to her husband and instantly he begins his rage and brutally beats her. While Bean and his sister stands there wailing for their mother, he places his hands over his sister's ears so she wouldn't hear the screams and cries from their mother. After the brutal beating, Bean's mother walks out of the room to comfort her children, pretending that she was okay saying, hey, Son, are you two ready to go? Bean looks at his mother with a look of empathy and anger at the same time, he noticed both of her eyes were swelling from the trauma of being brutal beaten by his stepdad and he becomes in rage and says, I swear I'm going to kill that nigga. Bean mom grabs him by the face and says, "Never let me hear you say that again." I know it looks bad, but he has a lot on his plate trying to take care of us. Bean replies he doesn't do shit for us and let him tell it, he doesn't care if we live or die, and Tai is his real daughter. Bean's mom unresponsive looks in a discouraging manner as Bean and Tai walk out the door to go to school. Then suddenly she yells out Bean, Bean looks back at his mother and she speaks. I hope you have a good day Son and I love you. Bean turns back around and continues his pathway to school. (As music is playing in the school halls.) Bean walks at an increasing pace as if he did not want to be seen going into his eighth-grade classroom, but as he walks to his seat some of his classmates begin to tease him about his clothing and shoes.... (Saying.) Look at this bum! The class starts laughing out loud, and then another classmate by the name of Brice says. Brah, look at his shoes, damn you poor as fuck. As Bean makes it to his seat, he makes eye contact with a female classmate by the name of Joy and puts his head down... The teacher sees the hurt on Bean's face and intervenes and says to the class and Brice ... Settle down, settle down I said, and you, Brice, have the Audacity to talk about somebody and have been sitting here in the eighth grade for 2 years straight... The entire class burst out into laughter which caused Brice to become embarrassed, and he says.. So what bitch, and I'm still getting paid. The teacher instantly yells, telling Brice, Get out of my classroom, with your little disrespectful self! You probably can't even spell the word. Brice gets up and walks to the door, grabs his private part, and tells the teacher...

Suck this... Brice partner in crime Jax laughs at Brice gesture towards the teacher.... Then the teacher tells Jax, you can leave also. Jax replies to the teacher and says, but I didn't do anything.

The teacher responds and speaks. Right, do you ever do, now, is there anyone else who needs to leave? The class responds no and becomes attentive to the teacher. The teacher brings the classroom back to order and responds. Now take out your textbook so we can go over the assignment for next week's test....

and with this assignment I am assigning partners. The classroom sighs and speaks out loud and replies, all man. The teacher begins assigning partners..

As the teacher continues to assign partners for the assignment, Bean looks towards the classroom feeling a sense of anxiety hoping the teacher has forgotten that he was in the classroom so he would not be paired with another student, then suddenly the teacher call's his name and he a disparaging look as if his life is about to end. then, he hears the teacher say. Bean you and Joy will be partners. Then suddenly Bean starts to feel his heartbeat in his throat beating rapidly until Joy looked over at him and smiled, giving Bean the ultimate relief of feeling that he was accepted by her regardless of his appearance. After class Joy walks up to Bean and asks. "Do you want to meet over your house or mines," Bean quickly responded as if he was petrified and spoke. Your house, Joy looked as if she said something wrong, then replied Okay! That's cool, but we have to get started soon so we can have time to prepare, is later today okay? Bean hesitated and said I don't know; I'll have to see. Joy replied again, okay! well here's my cell number, call me and let me know. Bean looked confused and spoke. I don't have a cell phone. Joy looks stunned and replies. That's okay, you can call me from your house phone.. Bean looks at Joy and puts his head down and says softly, "I don't have that either. Joy looks and feels a sense of empathy and speaks. Hey! don't worry about it, we will figure this out and come up with a solution, and tells Bean, I'll see you tomorrow. Bean replies okay, see you tomorrow and walks off. As Bean walks home he goes through a neighborhood that's full of gang bangers and drug dealers, then he is stopped by a known male by the name of Flex, and he speaks. What's up Lil Bean, I see you still hitting those books keeping yourself out of these streets. Huh? Bean shakes his head and agrees. Flex again responds and speaks. Well, aint nothing wrong with that, if that's how you choose to live, but from what I see, it aint doing shit for you Lil Bean. Flex looks Bean up and down and says, look at you man, your shoes all ran down and look like you still have on yesterday clothes, man that aint no way to live. Then another O'G male walks up by the name of "Bo" and tells Flex, man don't be corrupting the kid, let him be a kid and stay in school, so he can get a decent education. And then the O'G looks at Bean and says, Lil Bean, stay in school because these streets are not for everybody. Bean looks at the O'G in a sad manner, then Flex responds and tells the O'G, shut the fuck up, this my Lil homie, and I am just trying to look out for him like an O'G did for me. Look at this man, you can see he's starving and I'm just trying to help him eat. Flex pulls out a pocket full of money and gives Bean six hundred dollars and speaks. Now, if you're looking for more of that, you know where I'm at Lil Bean, now go buy yourself some shoes and a pair of new pants and keep the rest for lunch. Bean ecstatic takes the money and runs, and soon as he sees a shoe store he goes inside and buys himself a pair of shoes and a new pair of pants. As Bean walked up to his house and he noticed his mom and sister sitting outside, as he continued walking slowly he could feel a sense of discomfort and then his mom asked. Where have you been? Bean looks and replies. Nowhere. Bean mom looks at him and speaks. Boy, don't you lie to me, what's inside the bag? Bean opens and shows his mom and replies. A pair of shoes and pants. Bean mom responds. And where did you get them from? Bean looks with his head down and speaks. When I was walking home Flex stopped me, and gave me the money, and told me to go buy it. Bean mom looks and speaks. And son, what did you do to get them shoes and a pair of pants? Instantly Bean responds. Nothing! I didn't have to do anything, he said he was just looking out for me, like the O'G did him. Bean mom shakes her head in a sense of disgust and speaks. Son, aint nothing in this world for free, not even the air we breathe. Now, I hope you are happy, so I'm going to say this, and say this only once, stay away from Flex, do you hear me? Bean looks at his mom with his finger crossed behind his back and says Yes, I hear you. Bean walks inside the house and comes back out angrily and asks. The lights off again? Tai responds. Yes! And I'm hot and hungry. Bean walks out the door, slams it, and speaks. Not for long, I'll be right back. Bean mom looks and asks what do you mean not for long and where do you think you're going? Bean tells his mom as if he was a grown man. Look mom, Tai is hot and hungry and it's no telling when Mr. Todd is coming home, I have money left, so here take it, and pay the light bill and I'm going to go get food for you and Tai. Bean mom looks and speaks. No son, I will not allow you to do this. We will wait for Todd to come home, and he will fix everything. Bean yells unintentionally at his mom and speaks. Mom, when will you wake up, that man don't give a damn about us, why are you allowing us to live in these conditions, its hot in there and we are miserable. Bean mom looks saddened and agrees and allows Bean to go get the food while she pays the light bill.

Damn! It was a good day.

The next morning as Bean and his family wakes up Bean is overly excited and cannot wait to get to school to show off his new shoes and pants. He was so eager he was rushing his sister Tai to get ready so they would not be late. As he was walking out of his room, his mom looked at him and replied. Hmm! them some nice shoes son, you look very handsome, but it's not like you weren't before! Bean looked at his mom and smiled and spoke. Thanks mom. Oh yea, mom is it okay if I come home a little late, I have an assignment for class, and I am partnered up with a classmate and she asked could I go over to her house to complete it. Bean's mom and Tai looks at him smiles and speaks. Oh! Now I see why you are looking so fly and happy this morning. Bean looks and denies that it has anything to do with Joy and speaks. Naw Mom don't get me wrong; I mean she's pretty and all, but I don't think she would go for a guy like me, and anyway it's for school, that's it. Bean mom looks concerned and replies. What do you mean a guy like you, Son, you are a very handsome young man, and any girl would gladly be your girlfriend when the time is right, and to answer your question, you know I'm not going to say no, when it has anything to do with school. Bean looks and speaks. Thanks mom, I'll come home soon after.

When Bean walked inside his classroom you could see all eyes on him, and it became quiet as if the class were in a moment of silence. When Joy noticed Bean walking to his seat, she instantly smiled walking over to him just to say hello, then she told him, you look handsome today, sparking Bean to give off a smile and speak. Thank you, then he says, oh yea my mom said it will be okay for me to stay late after school to start on my assignment. Joy smiles and responds. Okay! Great, I'll see you after school. Bean replies. See you after school. As Bean walks to his seat Brice looks down at Bean expensive sneakers and blurts out in a jealous manner and speaks. nigga you still a bum. Bean looks at Brice and puts his two fingers up as if he had a gun and shoots at him making him become furious and Brice then says. Nigga whenever you ready, let's do this. The teacher yells out and speaks. Hey! Calm down, what is up with you two? Then she proceeded to teach her assignments. After class Bean and Joy met up at the school's library to go over their assignment. As Joy was going over the assignment she noticed Bean was bashful to read in front of her, so she took the initiative and lead, while Joy was engaged into the schoolwork, Bean was mesmerized by Joy intellect and mature demeanor, then Joy asked Bean who was in another dimension, do you understand what I just read? Bean looks lost and then gathers his thoughts and says, um, yea I understand. Joy politely smiles and says fine. After completing parts of their assignment, Joy noticed it was getting late and told Bean they would have to finish the rest tomorrow, because she had to go home early for her dad's birthday party. Bean looked shocked and asked. I know you hate that huh? Joy looks and asks. hate what, going home to my dad's birthday party? Bean looks and replies by nodding his head up and down and then answering yes. Joy looks undoubtful and speaks. Not at all, I have one of the best dads ever, and I love him so much. Then Joy looks at Bean and asks him "what about you? Bean looks and asks her "what about me? Then she replies. Meaning what about your dad? Bean looks angrily and says I don't have one. Joy looks, laughs, and asks. You don't have one or is your dad estranged from your home? Bean looks at Joy and asks. What do you mean by estranged? Joy explains herself and speaks. Did you ever meet your dad or is it that, he is not living under the same roof as you? Bean looks and says well I never met my real dad, he was killed when I was just a baby, and the guy who is married to my mom is my sister's dad, but we don't get along. Joy looks and feels a sense of empathy and speaks. Sorry to hear that, but hey, if you ever need a male role model, it's my dad, he is a pastor and he is always helping boys who didn't have a chance to be raised by their dads. Bean smirks and replies. A pastor, I don't believe in all that pastor stuff. Joy looks suspicious and asks. What are you saying, you don't believe in God? Bean looks at Joy trying to get around the question and speaks. Hey! I told my mom I would be home before dark, so I better be going. Joy looks and speaks. Okay, well we will pick up where we left off tomorrow. Bean looks, agrees, and speaks. Cool! tomorrow at the same time. Joy smiles and replies tomorrow at the same time. Bean gives Joy a thumbs up, and then Joy says...Hey! Bean, be safe out there. Bean looks, smiles, and speaks. Oh! Are you worried? Joy looks and speaks. Of course, I am. Bean looks and asks, why, everybody else seems not to like me. Joy responds and says, Well I'm not like everybody else and I believe under all that pain, there is a really nice guy who just have to give all his troubles to God.. Bean shakes his head, laughs, and speaks. Now, you sound like a pastor. Joy replies. Well, I'm a pastor daughter. Bean looks and tells Joy Goodnight and walks away.

It goes down in the hood.

As Bean makes his way home he ran into Brice and Jax, who were waiting on him on the street corner "where it all goes down" Brice walks up to Bean and instantly throws a punch trying to knock him out but misses. Bean looks around and sees that Jax is headed towards him to counteract, and Bean takes off running to escape. Bean ran so fast trying to dodge the two he ran straight into Flex almost knocking him flat on his back. Then Flex says. Damn Lil Bean you almost killed a nigga, who the fuck you running from like that? Bean barely can speak from being out of breath points in Brice and Jax direction as they were coming around the corner at top speed. Then Flex gets angry and tells Bean. Why the fuck are you running from them Lil niggas. Then Flex asks Brice and Jax, Lil niggas Ya have a problem with my Lil homie and pulls out his gun causing Brice and Jax to takeoff running and then throwing up their gang signs. Flex then tells Bean, "I see you got a little pressure on your hands, what did you do to them. Bean looks confused and replies. Nothing, they just don't like me.

After, Flex begins explaining to Bean. See, that's why you need someone like me to help protect your Lil ass, but don't worry I got you, lets walk over here. Flex walks Bean to his car and opens his trunk and pulls out a pistol and tries to hand it to Bean, but Bean was hesitant and showed fear, then Flex speaks. What the fuck are you scared of you need this shit for protection, and when those niggas try that shit again, you blaze one of their asses, now, here take it. Bean looks around and takes the gun and puts it in his pocket. Then Flex replies. Now, doesn't that make you feel secure? Bean grabs his pants pocket where the gun is and shakes his head and speaks. Yea, yea it does. Flex gives Bean a hand dap and tells him, you know you my Lil nigga and I got you, so whenever you're ready to see what this world can offer you other than that fake ass education, holla at me. Bean shakes his head in an agreement manner and walks off, then turns around and asks. Hey! Flex. Flex responds. What's up? Bean looks and asks. You think you can help me out with a cell phone. Flex looks, laughs, and pulls out a pocket full of money and replies. Help you out, Lil nigga how much you need? then says fuck it, here, take all this it's a grand? Bean's eyes become wide open as if he were in a state of shock to see so much money and speaks. All of it? Flex laughs and speaks. Yes Lil nigga, All of it. Bean looks and remembers what his mom said "Son aint nothing in this world for free" And then asks Flex, well what do I have to do to pay you back, I don't have a job. Flex looks and speaks. Not yet but you will, now get out of here. Bean takes the money and run home.

When Bean gets home he is greeted by his malicious stepdad, asking him, where the fuck you coming from this time of the night? Bean looks at him and doesn't respond and continue to walk past him. As he walked toward his room, he noticed his mom clinching and holding onto Tai tightly in her arms as if she was a newborn baby. Soon as Bean gets ready to open his mouth, his stepdad punches him in the back of the head and replies. Boy! Don't you walk away and disrespect me when I ask your ass a question, answer me Lil nigga. Instantly Bean grabs his pocket in rage causing his stepdad to back down and walk away. Bean then ran over to his mom and Tai and asked his mom, "What's wrong with

Tai, His mom continually clinched on to Tai in tears, then again he asks, mom, what's wrong with Tai? Tai looks at Bean with tears in her eyes, showing him signs that the very man who fathered her had committed a hateful and cruel act upon her causing her emotional and physical damage. "Todd had sexual abused his own daughter." Bean begins to cry and tells Tai, "I'm sorry sister for not being here to protect you, I'm so sorry. Then Bean's mom tells him, no son, you're not to blame, I am, it's all my fault.. Then Bean looks at his mom with a vicious stare and replies. Yes, it is your fault! And storms at his stepdad like a raging bull. Causing his mom to jump between the two.

In a cowardly stare, Todd looks at Tai and his wife as if he felt a sense of remorse and speaks. For what it's worth, my father did the same thing to me, and I was younger than you, and I lived, so, you will live too. Bean looks at his mom and storms towards the door and stops. Todd then walks over and tries to comfort them causing his wife to scream out and respond, take your fucking hands off my baby. Then she stares Todd deep into his eyes and speaks. If you ever touch her again I swear to God, I will kill you with my bare fucking hands. Bean standing in the doorway hears the brutal words coming out of his mom's mouth and for once in his lifetime, he felt a sense of relief, that his mom finally had enough of Todd shit and was ready to go to war to protect her children from a brutal man.

Todd sees the seriousness in his wife's face and back away grabbing his hat and keys and as he walks past Bean heading out the door, he stops and looks back and replies. Fuck all Ya. And slammed the door. Tai cries out and speaks, my own daddy hurt me Mommie, he hurt me, I don't ever want to see him again. Bean standing there with tears in his eyes, takes off running out of the as fast as he can. Prompting his mom to yell his name as if she knew he was up to no good. Bean! Bean, she screams please son, but Bean kept on running as fast as he could, until he came to a dark alley falling down and burying himself into a small corner to get tranquility.

Before Bean knew it, he had woken up in a dark alley where bums and dope fiends gather provokingly causing him to jump up quickly to hurry home. As Bean starts to walk he hears a familiar voice, stops, and hides. When Bean sees that it was his stepdad, his heart begins pounding as if a drummer was beating on a drum and instantly becomes in rage, remembering all the pain and turmoil he has caused his family and to add more puncture to his wounds, the thought of Todd hurting his beloved baby sister made him even more furious. As Todd walks through the dark alley Bean sneaks up behind him and calls out his name. Todd! Todd turns around and sees that its Bean and responds. What the fuck are you doing here, Lil nigga? Are you following me or something? Then Bean pulls out his pistol aiming it at Todd causing Todd to laugh it off and asks. So, what the fuck are you going to do with that, you aint no killer. You're softer than a newborn baby. It should've been you I fucked, and starts laughing, Bean and Todd stares at each other and then Todd holds his hands up and says, look Lil nigga, I had a long night, and I'm tired. I'm going home to be with my beautiful family, are you coming? Bean looks without saying a word, then Todd turns around, with his back facing Bean and speaks. Fuck you then nigga. Bean replay's the last thing he heard his sister say "I don't ever want to see him again" closed his eyes and Boom! Pulls the trigger. Causing Todd to fall to his knees. Then Bean walks over to Todd while he was on his knees and says, I never liked you anyway Bitch ass nigga and pulls the trigger again, shooting Todd in the back of his head splattering blood all over his clothes. Then Bean looks at Todd lifeless body on the ground becomes fearful and takes off running making it to the corner where the O'G Flex operates. When Bean sees Flex he runs up to him looking frighten as can be, Flex looks at Bean as if he saw a ghost and saw that Bean clothes was drenched with blood and jumps up and tells him instantly go into my house now! Once Flex gets Bean into the house he looks at Bean and asks him, Lil nigga who you done killed? Bean looks up at Flex in an empathy stare and remains speechless. For a moment it was like Flex read his mind and already knew it was his stepdad by the tears in his eyes from feeling remorseful, as he did when he too had to do the very same thing. Feeling a sense of compassion, Flex tells Bean to take off his clothes and get his ass in the shower, then tells Bean, we have to burn these fucking clothes. Then he asked Bean in a concerned tone, "Do you still have the gun? Bean shows him the gun and Flex says, yea we have to get rid of that too, we can't leave any evidence. After Bean gets out of the shower Flex shows Bean how to discard of his bloody clothes and the murder weapon and then Drives him home. As they sat in the car, Flex tries to encourage Bean by saying, look I know you are a cool ass Lil nigga, that's why I fucks with you, and for what it's worth, you did what you had to do to protect your family. The question is, now that you did, how are you going to man up and take care of them, are you ready to stand in the paint for them, and be that man they need you to be? Bean looks at Flex and replies. Do I have any other choices? Flex looks at Bean and shakes his head and tells him. The way I see it, No. Bean then gets out of the car and continues to walk away and suddenly, Flex speaks and says, I'll see you tomorrow, welcome to the game and pulls off.

When Bean walked into the house his mother was standing there waiting for him, and as he tries to walk past her, she stops him and asks. Son, where have you been all night? Bean just stares at his mom, wishing and craving for her comfort as she once used to give, before when he has done something wrong. She looked into Bean's eyes and saw that he was troubled and suddenly grabbed him embracing him tightly and began to cry out and says to him "I'm sorry, I'm so sorry son. Causing Bean to break down in tears.

A made killer.

The next morning Bean was up and ready for school, feeling a sense of remorse but relieved on the other hand, that they no longer had to deal with Todd ever again. As he walks into the kitchen his mother is standing there, then suddenly she asks, Bean, where did you go last night? Bean looks with his head bowed down and answers untruthfully and says, nowhere really, I just walked around to clear my head. Then she asks, who was that in the car last night? Then Bean looked hesitant because he remembers what his mom said about Flex, then she asked him, was it Flex? Bean just stared as if he was lost in space, not wanting his mom to feel that he intentionally disobeyed her. Then she says, look, I have enough on my plate dealing with Todd and I don't want any more problems son, why can't you stop being bullheaded and listen to me for once. Then Bean answers and says, Listen to what? Flex helps me, he is the only one that seems to care about me around here, besides Tai. Then his mom yells, care about you or baiting you to be his next victim, son wake up, he doesn't care about you, he's using you. Then Bean becomes angry and speaks. Using me, if it weren't for him, we wouldn't have these lights on, or food to eat, Bean mom interrupts and says, that's not true, now no matter how bad Todd is, he wouldn't let us go for long period without lights or food. Then

Bean yells out and says, Forget Todd, is that all you ever worry about, is making him happy, all the nasty things he did to us and raping his own daughter, why you did nothing about it. Then instantly, feeling offended by what Bean said, she slaps him in the face and says, now one thing I will not tolerate, is you talking to me out of line. Now I know Todd isn't perfect, but he is still my husband, and he is going through a hard time. When he gets back…Bean yells out, he's not coming back, he is never coming back, to hurt me or Tai ever again. Bean Mom looked as if her heart stopped beating for a minute and shockingly asked Bean, what do you mean about that? Bean looked at his mom with hurt and anger but couldn't bring himself to terms with telling her what he meant.

Then she says. Bean, son, look at me, did you do something to Todd? Answer me! Then Bean looked at his mom, and with all his might said, no, no I didn't. Then Bean mom looked as if she was revived, and her heart began beating once again and asked Bean why did you say that? Then Bean looked at his mom and told her some off the wall story that, he saw Todd get into another woman's vehicle with some of his personal belongings as if he was moving away. And for that moment, I felt relieved and happy because, I thought finally, we can get back to being a family without him, without him ever hurting one of us again. Bean mom looked at him and burst into tears and when he went towards her to console her, she quickly refrained from shedding tears as if for a moment she felt a sense of relief and peace. As she started to do her daily routine, she took dinner out to prepare for tonight's meal, she told him and Tai to go on to school and have a good day and she would be fine.

Never can say goodbye.

When Bean returned to school, the look on his face was as if he had been up all night on someone's nine to five, as he made his way to the hallways he saw Joy standing by the staircase looking elated as always. Joy sympathetically looks at Bean and noticed that he didn't look like the Bean she saw on yesterday and quickly made her way over to him asking, is everything okay? Then Bean looked and said, it will be. Joy looked puzzled and asked what do you mean by will be? Bean told Joy he didn't have time to talk, and they will talk later. He just came to tell her that he will not be back in school for a while, but he really likes her and wanted to say goodbye. Then Joy looked at him and said what do you mean say goodbye, are you moving away or something? Bean looked at her and said no, and that it was complicated to explain now, but he promised he would one day. Bean walked up to Joy giving her a hug and said goodbye. As he turned to walk away, Joy grabbed his hand and spoke. It's never goodbye, this isn't final, I'm here and I will always be. Then the bell rings and the teacher call out for Joy and Bean to come inside of the class and as Bean begins to walk away, Joy yells out his name, Bean! Then Bean turns around, Joy runs up to him and gives him a hug and then suddenly passionately kisses and tells him to be safe and they will talk soon. Then Bean runs out of the school and heads to Flex house. Once Bean reaches Flex house, the O'G opens the door and welcomes Bean inside. Flex begins to explain the game, telling him this is the only way he sees fit for him to help his family financially. Also telling Bean he can always go back to school, but for now, he has to be the man that his stepdad never showed him how to be for his family. Bean looked at Flex and asked him, how do I do that? Flex then says, "I'm glad you asked, Flex walks Bean to a closed room door in his house and opens the door to a room filled with narcotics and naked women and responded with, by selling this.

Bean Mom gets a shocking revelation.

When Bean returns home and hits the corner he is startled by the police at his house, he then stops suddenly and starts to panic and just as he begins to turn around to walk away, his mom sees him and calls out to him in a sorrowful tone, Bean! As she cries profusely, Todd is dead. Bean looks as if he was in a state of shock, reacting as if he were unaware and begins to console his mom asking her, what happened to him? Then his mom tells him, the police say it was a possible robbery and someone shot him dead. Bean felt a sense of comfort and began to tell his mom. Don't worry mom, I promise we will be fine. I will take care of us.

From a boy to a man.

A few years have passed, and Bean is now 20 years of age. He has been living up to his responsibilities by taking care of his mom and sister. Standing on the corner alongside of Flex he has earned his badges of becoming a killer and showing loyalty to the one man who adopted him as his very own street son. It is evidently heard that, Bean name is playing a significant role in the operation of drug dealing and street crimes, gang banging that is, throughout the community as one of the most feared and respected drug dealers that's in the game thus far. "Flex taught him well."

As Bean stands there on the street corner next to his luxury car, he sees an old school rivalry Jax. Jax sees Bean and walks up to him and speaks. Hey! Bean, what's up man. Bean looks at him with a distasteful smirk on his face and replies. Who the fuck is this nigga? Jax replies. It's me Jax, from middle school, remember. Bean looks at him up and down and says oh! Yea, I remembered when you and your homie use to clown me and oh yeah, tried to beat me up. Jax looks unease and says, that's when we were younger, man kids do foolish things, but now we're all grown up and plus I changed my life around. I'm a saved man. I gave my life to God. Bean looks at Jax and burst out into laughter and replies. And who saved you, this supposed to be God, you all talk so much about? Jax responds. And speaks. Yes! yes God and he can save you as well. Bean tells Jax I don't need your God to save me, I had to save my damn self, from niggas like you and your homie. Jax looks at Bean and sees the anguish in his eyes and becomes nervous and tells Bean Okay, nice seeing you again, I better be going, it gets pretty dark around here, and I don't like to be out this late. Bean looks at Jax and asks. But you say you have your God right? Jax looks at Bean and says, no, God has me, and walks away. Bean standing there with his crew tells them the story of being bullied by Jax and Brice and says, do you believe this nigga chased me with his Lil homie and tried to put down on me? Bean crew begins to laugh and as Bean reminisces he becomes angry and sees Jax making his way to the next street corner and begins to chase him down, When Jax turns around he sees Bean headed towards him and takes off running contemplating an escape but runs into a dead-end. Bean then pulls out his gun and asks Jax, while breathing heavily from the chase, you said God got you right? Jax looks at Bean, smiles, and says wholeheartedly he does. Then Bean aims the gun close range to Jax face and tells him, "Well go to him then, nigga" And shoot Jax between his eyes killing him instantly.

A stone-cold murderer.

The next morning the word on the streets is Bean is out of control and has killed an innocent young man. This caused an uproar throughout the community prompting for justice. However, the police claims show there is no substantial evidence that Bean took part in such a crime. “Even the police feared him.” When Bean returned home his mom was so heartbroken from the news she asked Bean. Son, did you have anything to do with taking that young man’s life? Bean looks at his mom straight in the eyes and said, of course not mom, I would never do anything like that. Bean mom looks at him and replies. Son, I know I might not have been the perfect mother, but I did my best to raise you right. Now, if you had anything to do with taking that boy's life you will have to deal with God. Bean suddenly becomes agitated and says, please spare me with this God shit, like I told you before, I didn't have anything to do with that nigga getting killed. Damn! I just hope everybody leaves me alone and walks out the door slamming it.

On the way back to the corner Bean gets a call from Flex, Bean answers by saying, talk to me Boss. Flex responds, young nigga what did you do now, man I have all the O'G's calling me up saying you killed some holy nigga that was well known in the community for doing good deeds. Bean tells Flex, well, he wasn't good a few years ago, that's the same nigga who chased me down the streets when I was in middle school trying to beat my head in. Flex replies, I knew if you did it, it was for a good reason. You know the motto "Once an Opp, always an Opp" You did what I taught you to do, and I stand behind you one hundred percent. This life we live, you only have two choices. "Kill or be Killed." Bean agrees and replies. Respect to you, Bossman. Flex then tells Bean; I want you to do something for me. Bean replies. Anything Boss. Flex continues and says, I want you to lay low for a while until this thing cools down. Bean replies. No disrespect Boss, but I'm not afraid of none of those niggas. Flex laughs out loud and responds. I know, I know young nigga, but do it just for me, I mean sometimes it's okay to have a little fun, get you a nice girl and go to one of those expensive hotels and chill, at least until they lay that Lil nigga to rest. Bean replies. Who is going to run the operation? Flex replies. Don't worry about all that, just do what I ask of you and let me take care of the rest. Bean replies. Ok Boss. Flex and Bean hangs up the phone at the same time. Bean sits and thinks about what Flex asked of him so he decided to give Joy a call, but when Joy answered the phone you could hear in her voice that she had been crying. Then Bean speaks and says, hey bae, what's going on? Out of the blue Joy is straightforward and asks the question that has been pondering in her head all night. Bean, is it true what they are saying, that you were the one who killed Jax? Bean sounding baffled as if he believed his own lie and tells Joy baby no, it's not true. Then he rephrases his answer and says, well kind of. Joy replies in a disappointing tone. What do you mean kind of? Bean being the perfect example of what cunning is, puts on a perfect show and speaks. I feel so bad baby for him, I really tried to stop him, but I couldn't. Joy tells Bean, Baby you are confusing me, stop who? Then Bean says, I know who killed Jax, but I can't say. Bean pretends to cry and tells Joy, Baby, I saw the whole thing and now Flex wants me to go and hide out at a hotel, just until things have settled down. Joy replies, Bean are you telling me the truth? Bean responds baby you know you all I have; I would never lie about something like this. Then Joy says, well I agree with Flex, I think you should go to a hotel, at least until they find the person or people who did such a heinous crime to a God-fearing man. Bean then says, I will not go unless you go with me, Joy then tells Bean, you know I am in school, I can't just stop school like that, my dad will be furious, Then Bean tells Joy, you don't have to stop school baby, just be there with me that's all I asks, please! I need you right now. Joy responds, Okay! Let me gather some things and I will call you when I'm ready. While Joy is home gathering some things, Bean is on the phone talking to his crew telling them that he is going to lay low until all the hiatus about the murder of Jax has cooled down. Telling them once he is settled, he will call and give them the details of his whereabouts. After Bean gets off the phone with his crew, he gets in his car and drives heading to his mom's house to pick up some belongings for his extended stay at the hotel, Bean gets out of the car and is stopped by one of his clients by the name of No-good, No-good yells out. Bean! what's up, let me hold something. Bean responds in a joking manner and tells him to hold these nuts. then No-good, asks about the situation that's circulating between him and Jax. Is it true what they are saying? Bean looks at No-good in an awry manner and asks, what who is saying? No-good responds, that you ran down on Jax. Bean looks and asks, who told you that shit? No-good tells Bean, the streets are talking. Bean responds and says, well, let them continue to talk and if that's what they are saying, then that's what it is. I'm tired of people thinking he was a saint, that nigga got just want he deserves. No-good then tells Bean, well you know what they say, when you live by the sword, nigga you gone die by that bitch as well. Bean looks at No-good and responds, well I tell you this, when it's my time to go, I hope them niggas, don't show me no mercy. Because I have none, to show. No-good looks at Bean and replies, damn! you are a coldhearted nigga. Bean looks at No-good and asks, What the fuck you want anyway. No-good tells Bean I was headed on the block to get some of that good, good but I ran into you right here. Bean tells No-good, Nigga you know I don't get down like that around my mom's crib. No-good apologizes and then Bean tells him, look I'm going to lay low for a minute and take my girl to one of these fancy hotels, and just chill, so come by and I got you. And come alone, I don’t need people to know where I’m at.

No-good tells Bean, no problem my mouth is zipped.

Bean goes into Hiding.

While Bean waits for Joy he sits on the bed and starts counting his money and then there is a knock at the door. (Knock, knock knock) Bean grabs his gun and yells in an aggravating voice. Who is it? No-good replies it's me looking zoned out. Bean jumps up to go answer the door and looks through the peephole and asks, what the fuck you want now? No-good (Staggering) replies, I need one. Bean quickly opens the door and tells No-good, Nigga don't be saying that shit out loud, and damn, didn't you just leave? No-good shrugs his shoulder and Bean responds. Man come in. Bean walks back to retrieve the drugs for No-Good as No-good walks behind him and speaks. Hey man, I know you don't credit. Bean cuts No-good off and speaks. You damn right I don't credit. No Good looking desperate and begins scratching parts of his body and replies. Look man, I need it. And I don't get paid until Friday, but I swear I'll pay you back then. Bean gets angry and replies. What are you fucking deaf or something, Bitch I said I don't credit. And you banging on my fucking door like you the fucking POPO, and now you are telling me, you don't even have no money. No-good falls to his knees and begins to plead. Please! Bean, come on man I'll pay you with interest. Bean looks at No-good in a disgusted manner and speaks, Man, get your ass up, begging and shit. No-good jumps up apologetic and says, I'm sorry, but I need it bro. Bean looks and asked. Nigga, this shit that good. No-good looks at Bean with an undeniable stare and says, it’s to die for. Bean looks seriously at No-good and begins to laugh and replies, Nigga you better not be a minute late with my bread, I have a fucking business to run. No-good looking grateful and speaks. I promise, I won’t. Then Bean gives No-good the drugs and tells him. And don't be telling no body I gave you credit, I have a reputation to live up to nigga. No-good looks and replies. I won't, and then asks Bean, can I have two. Bean looks and screams. Nigga! hell no. No-good runs away and then Bean speaks out to himself. Damn! these niggas are really crack fiends. Bean goes back and sits on the bed and begin to roll up a blunt and a commercial comes on about drugs. (This is your brain on drugs). Bean laughs out loud and says, Now, that's why I say no to drugs. (Laughing and smokes his blunt) Bean gets up and goes to the kitchen to pour himself a drink when he turns around, he sees an imaginary ghost figure that frightens him and he panics and says, What the fuck? Then he shakes it off and talks to himself once again asking, what the fuck in this drink ... got me tripping.... As Bean walks back to his bed, he hears another commercial with a male voice asking, do you believe in God? (Bean begins to laugh and answers.) Umm! No, not your fake ass God, The Pastor on tv (emphasizes) If you don't get yourself together you are going straight to Hell!! Bean disagrees and says, well, I have news for you

Pastor, we might be already here. (lol) Stupid, there's no such thing as Heaven or Hell. Then Bean walks over to the tv and changes the channel, while smoking on his blunt his phone rings and he answers, Hello. It's Joy. Hey Bae. Bean in an angry tone speaks. Bae my ass, where the fuck are you? Joy looks at the phone in an annoying way. Umm, excuse me, you already know where I'm at, I told you I had to get some things before I come there. Bean looks at his watch and replies, but you didn't tell me you had to go out shopping to get those things. Joy responds, um! I'm going to an expensive hotel, at least let me feel like I belong there. Bean replies with, whatever just hurry up and stop trying to buy out the fucking mall? Joy looks at the phone laughs, and says, don't flatter yourself you didn't send me that much money. Anyway, I was calling to tell you, I'll catch a uber when I'm on my way. Bean begin smiling and grabbing his Penis and tells Joy, Well hurry your ass up baby; daddy got a big surprise for you. Joy becomes submissive and replies, Ok daddy, on the way. Bean hangs up the phone and begins to feel high from the blunt and mumbles, damn! A nigga feeling the 2 H's high and horny. As Bean waits for his girl, he reaches over and grabs his phone and calls a male companion on facetime, then he answers with an attitude, Yes Bean. What do you want? Bean responds and asks, What the fuck you mean what do I want, you don't want to see me? Male companion replies, boy, you play too many games, so why waste my precious time seeing you? Bean pulls out his Penis and begins to ejaculate and tells his male companion, So, you can suck on this. And then his male companion becomes excited and says, damn! Daddy, it's so big, I want it, I want it. Bean then tells him, open your mouth... Then the male companion tells Bean, give it to me daddy.... Bean begins to moan as he ejaculates over the phone. Aww! Open, here it comes. The male companion moans in a sexual tone saying, damn, damn baby when you...... Then Bean quickly hangs up the phone on his male companion and speaks. Shut the fuck up Faggot! Bean gets up and cleans off his phone, rolls over, falls asleep, and begins dreaming. In Bean dream he goes to an unknown place. As he begins to walk inside the building he asks himself, Where the fuck am I? Then he continues to walk down a long hallway and suddenly he comes to a door, as he begins to open it, he hears this voice saying. I wouldn't open that if I were you. Then Bean suddenly looks around, sees an unknown man, and then responds, Well that's the difference between you and me. I would. The unknown male begins to laugh and replies, you must be new here. Bean looks around puzzled and says, Naw! I'm not new nowhere, actually I'm well-known everywhere I go, but since you asked, where is here? The unknown male gives out a grimy laughter and says, here is where we check in. Bean looks around and says, check in, I don't check in nowhere. The unknown male looks at Bean and replies. I see. As Bean continues to walk he asks the unknown male. And what is this place, some kind of upscale hotel?

The unknown male looks and says, somewhat. I guess you can say that. Bean looks annoyed and tells the unknown male move the fuck out my way. The unknown male moves out of Bean way. Then suddenly Bean laughs and speaks. If you don't mind, I'm going to finish checking out the scenery. Bean begins walking around the unknown place and spots several doors and says, Shit! This has to be one of the biggest spookiest hotels I have ever seen. Again, Bean hears noise ahead and says, that sounds like my kind of music, so Bean follows the sound and when he approaches the door, he opens it. (Bean face begins to light up from the excitement and replies.) Damn! Ok, ok! I'm into that girl-on-girl action, party over here. How do I get down? The woman in the room continues to take part with their task. While Bean stands there and admire the beautiful women he speaks boldly. damn girl, I got something for all ya. Then again the same unknown male tells him. You can't be here. Bean again becomes agitated and asks, why not? you're here, and then Bean becomes angry and asked the unknown male, why the fuck you keep following me? The unknown male with a distinct gesture tells him, It's my Job. Bean gets annoyed and responds. Your Job! who the fuck hired you because it wasn't me. And what the fuck is your Job, to harass me? The unknown male assures him and says, no, not to harass you, but to make sure you're in the right room. Bean looks and says to the unknown male. The right room, I didn't reserve no fucking room and you don't have to make sure shit for me. I'm a grown ass man, and I can take care of myself. The unknown male agrees by saying. I saw that, and you did a great job I may say. Bean instantly stops and speaks. You talk like you know me or something. The unknown male looks at Bean and laughs with a serious stare and replies. Oh! that I do, now are you sure you don't need me to show you to your room? Been becomes aggravated and speaks. How many times I'm going to tell your ass, I didn't reserve a damn room. The unknown male informs Bean It was already reserved for you. Bean gets angry this time pulling out his gun and says look brah, I don't know what the fuck you're talking about, but somebody is going to die today. The unknown male begins to laugh as he walks away and replies. Oh! That’s for sure. Bean then looks hysterical begins to panic and says, I don't know what type of freaky ass game you're playing, but you're fucking with the wrong one. Bean begins walking down the hallway and ran into an occupied room full of familiar gang bangers, dope dealers, and as he scanned the room he spotted a gang banger he killed and says, damn that looks like, naw can’t be, I'm definitely tripping, and he continues and sees another man as he is walking up to the unknown man and asks. Hey brah, how do you get out of here? The unknown man asked him. What! Are you lost? Bean starts shaking his head in agreement. Yea, yea! I guess you can say that, and now I'm trying to find my way back out of here. The room gets silent, and everyone begins to stare awkwardly, and someone replies and speaks. Brah there's no way out once you're here you can't leave. Bean looks terrified and speaks. What the fuck you mean, I can't leave, where the fuck am I, where am I, where am I. Bean begins running up to people screaming pleading for help. How do you get out of here? Asking people frantically, help me somebody, help me please! Bean begins pacing, panicking and speaks. I got to get the fuck out of here. Bean sees someone that resembles No-good and yells No-good and begins to feel a sense of relief as he calls out. No-good name, No-good. Then No-good turns around and sees Bean and speaks. Hey! Bean, you, here too. Bean looks confused and speaks. Yea! I'm here too, but I'm trying to get out of here, where is the way out, I'm trying to get back home. No-good looks at Bean and shakes his head in a disappointing way and responds Bean, there's no way out. Bean again looks confused and speaks. What the fuck do you mean there's no way out? No-good explains. I mean, you can’t go home. And why the fuck not? Bean asked. No-good then informs Bean, because this is home, this is the end. Bean looks confused and asks, the end of what, what the fuck are you talking about? No-good looks at Bean sadly and informs Bean, because we're dead, we are in Hell. Bean looks around in shock and begins screaming. What! Do you mean we're dead? No-good looks at Bean and speaks. Yes, we all are. Bean begins to cry out.. I'm dead this can't be. No, No, No. I'm not dead, I'm not dead. While Bean is dreaming Joy, walks in the door and hears Bean screaming, she begins shaking him to wake him up. Bean, Bean, baby wake up, wake up you're dreaming. "**BEAN WAKES UP FROM HIS DREAM AND BEGINS SCREAMING.**" I'm not dead, I'm not dead. Joy then asked Bean, "What are you talking about, wake up, wake up. Bean wakes up crying out. Bae, Bae help me! Joy panickily shakes Bean saying Baby I'm right here, wake up baby, come on snap out of it. Bean gasping for his breath barely can talk. Baby, Baby! Joy responds, yes, I'm right here. Bean begins looking around and asks. Where am I, am I home? Joy looks sympathetic. Yes, your home, baby What the fuck is going on with you? Bean jumps up out of bed and starts looking around grabbing himself and begins to calm himself.

then Joy asks. What just happened? Bean tries to brush it off... and responds with nothing, nothing I'm alright, I just..... Then Bean stops and Joy shows a sense of concern and asks. You just what? Talk to me. Bean tries to change the subject and responds. brah... I just need a glass of water... Joy gets Bean a drink of water. As he drinks the water he begins to feel a sense of relief prompting Joy to ask, are you ready to tell me what just happened? Bean in a dreadful state says, Bae, I said it was nothing why are you tripping? Joy explains to Bean. No that was something and it's happening more often. Bean looks with reassurance and speaks. Look, I just keep having these weird ass dreams that....

Joy interrupts and says, “What that your dead? Bean looks nervous and speaks arrogantly...and responds, Yeah, that I'm dead... but I'm not dead baby...I'm not dead... Joy looks strangely at Bean and speaks. Um! It’s obvious you’re not because you’re standing right in front of me. Bean tries to calm down and replies, well okay then... Joy sighs and walks away...Bean apologizes and replies. come on bae...let's not do this, I'm okay... Joy looks fearful and speaks.... Bae you’re freaky me out, Now, I don't know what's going on or what you got yourself into. But these are not normal dreams. Where I'm from growing up in the church with a praying grandmother and a father that’s a pastor, what I have encountered, baby these are warnings of destruction. Bean begins shaking his head and grabs his blunt and speaks, Omg! Not this again, damn I said its nothing... Joy gets upset and stares at Bean. Bean pleads with Joy and says, I need a blunt please! Joy grabs the blunt out of Bean mouth and says, you don't need a damn blunt that's the problem now. You need to stop smoking. Bean agrees and speaks. Yeah! You right bae, I need to stop smoking but not now. Joy walks away and replies. Whatever! I'm leaving, Bean grabs Joy and tells her. Don't leave me please. Bean starts kissing Joy causing her to get heated then Joy begins to moan and says, hmm! You act like you miss me. Bean replies I do, now let me show you just how much. Bean goes down kissing Joy's vagina while enjoying the intimacy, she suddenly stops Bean and asks. Wait a minute, where's my big surprise? Bean pulls down his pants and pulls out his penis and speaks. I'm glad you asked, it's right here baby. Joy inhales as he begins pushing his Penis deep inside of her. After the act while lying in bed, Bean compliments Joy and says, damn! That shit was good then Joy gets and ask, why do you have to call my pussy shit?

Bean looks, shakes his head and replies, I'm not calling your pussy shit, I said your pussy is the shit. Bean and Joy burst out with laughter. Joy then replies, Bae I'm hungry, let's go out and get something to eat? Bean replies, Yea me too, but you know I can't leave. Those streets are too hot right now for a young boss like me. Joy gets upset and says, see this what I am talking about, is this the type of life you want to live? sitting in a hotel room hiding because of your bad decisions by helping others destroy people's lives? Bean looks carefree and replies, Hell yeah, that's how I survive and let me remind you, that's how I keep you happy. Joy looks baffled and says, "Keep me happy, and how is that? Bean sighs and replies, by sending you on expensive shopping sprees. Joy responds quickly and says, now that's untrue, and let me remind you, I have my own money,

And do you really think that shopping is the only thing that makes me happy? Bean looks at Joy with an awkward look and says, Um Yea! Joy replies and says, well your mistaken, it's so much more that can make me happy. Bean questioned Joy and asked her, "Like what? Joy gets serious and responds, like giving all this up. Baby, there is so much more out there in this world for you to grasp and enjoy. Bean smirks and speaks. What do you mean, I enjoy my life. Now tell me what can be better than not having to worry about where's your next meal is coming from, not having to answer to no one because you're your own boss, baby, look at me, I have money, jewelry, and a fancy car, plus I have one of the finest chicks on my side. Now, tell me what more I can ask for. Joy shakes her head in a disappointing manner and replies. Everlasting life, life without being fearful that someone is going to snatch that fake ass chain from around your neck, and a life in which you don't have to worry about the police pulling up on you because they suspect you are a drug dealer and lastly, a life without looking over your shoulders, thinking your Opp’s is coming back to put a bullet in your head. Bean looks while walking away and tells Joy. Man go ahead on with all that crazy shit. Joy replies. Okay! I'll go, but just remember this, the deeds that you do, will be done unto you. One day you're going to have to pay for all this, if not, God. Bean cuts her off and yells. God! Don't give me that God stuff, because I don’t care to hear it. You can believe in this Almighty God, because unfortunately you didn’t have a life like mines. So, believe in your God, while I believe in these streets. Joy continues her stance and says, you are damn right I believe, until the day he comes to take me to rest. Bean angrily questioned Joy, asking her where God was when my baby sister own father raped her, huh! and all I could do was just stand there and watch tears fall from her eyes because my mom was too afraid to do something about it. Do you know as a kid I had to stand there and watch that man beat the hell out of my mom, and she took it just so we can have a fucking roof over our heads. And if there was a God, why do he allow innocent kids to suffer and cry themselves to sleep because they don’t know where their next meal is coming from, tell me that? so I don't want to hear nothing else about your so-called God.

A few minutes later another commercial comes on with the same pastor preaching stating, God created Heaven and Hell? Bean gets mad and throws an object at the tv and speaks. Not you again, get the fuck off my tv, this is the last time I'm going to say this, Heaven and Hell are not real, you know why because there is no God, do you hear me, there is no God. Bean begins to start acting erratic tearing and smashing things to the floor and Joy begins to scream and cry, telling Bean to stop, please stop, you're scaring me. Bean looks, stops, and consoles Joy and tells her, Baby, I'm sorry, I'm sorry. Joy begins to speak. And tells Bean let's just stop, okay! We don't have to go out, I'll get the food and come back, and we can do what we always do, watch some of our favorite movies and play some board games, how does that sound? Bean shaking his head in agreement. Yea, that sounds good baby. Joy tells Bean okay; I'll be back soon. Bean watches his girlfriend walk to the door with a hurtful stare and speak. Bae! Joy stops and answers with a sad look. Yes. Bean tells Joy, I love you. Joy smiles and replies back. I love you too, but God loves you more and walks out the door. Bean turns his head and stands there with a stare, and his phone rings. It's Bean crew from the block. Hey! Bean, where are you? Bean replies, Lockdown, why! What's good? You heard about your boy? Bean looks concerned. Heard what? Your boy, Flex got hit up. Bean was stunned and started to break down, what do you mean hit up, is he alright, please tell me he's okay! Bean crew from the block answers.

From what they are saying it looks pretty bad. Bean drops his phone, then Bean crew from the block asked, are you still there? Bean regains his composure and answers, Yea I'm here. Who did this shit

They say it's retaliation from preacher boy you dropped, say if they couldn't get you, they would get Flex. Bean eyes tears up and then he says, I'm going to kill all of them nigga's before they get me. but hey, you know how this shit goes, A bullet for a bullet. Give my regards to his girl. And hang up the phone.

Bean meets the Devil.

After, Bean hangs up the phone he begins to pace and then breaks down. Bean does something that he never did before, he takes a few of his own drugs. Then he begins to feel drowsy then gets up for water and suddenly he collapses having an outer body experience. Bean sees his body lying face down on the floor and panics saying, What the fuck? Bean tries to wake himself up. Wake up, man wake the fuck up! Suddenly Bean turns and sees a man standing behind him and he asks, how the fuck did you get in my room? The unknown male replies. I'm everywhere. Then Bean asks him. What the fuck you want? The unknown male firmly says, I come for you. Bean gets aggressive turns around and tries to walk away.. and speaks. What! The fuck you mean come for me, man I'm not going nowhere with you

Bean then tries to walk back to his body and suddenly the unknown male grabs Bean and speaks in a demonic voice. The unknown male tells Bean, it's time to go. Bean screaming and fighting to keep his stance. Screaming and fighting as hard as he can. No, no let me go. Suddenly the unknown male and Bean vanishes into a dark room, Bean breathing heavily and asks. Where am I, where am I? The unknown male replies. Welcome back! Bean replies, please! You have the wrong guy. The unknown male begins laughing, and questioned Bean, the wrong guy. Oh no! I have the right guy, you're one of my best servants. The unknown male reveals himself as the devil and Bean gets hysterical and cries. The Devil begins laughing profusely. Joy walks into the room and sees Bean passed out on the floor, she drops the food, and runs over to him pleading for him to get up. Baby, baby, what have you done, get up baby, please.

She runs over to the refrigerator to retrieve milk for him to drink, as she returns she turns him over to help him try to drink it. Joy (screaming) Bean, please come on baby you have to drink this. She then begins to pull his lifeless body into the bathroom and gets him into the shower and turns on the water. Bean on his knees crying out. Asking Please, let me go. The Devil tells Bean, even if I could, why would I, I have no dominion over death, I only can manipulate and control you through your thoughts, it was you who acted out on it by accepting me as your God. Bean quickly denies his acceptance, I never accepted you. The Devil turns, looks, and speaks. Oh yes you did, you might not have accepted me with your tongue, but you accepted me by your actions. Bean tells the devil he disagrees, and the devil tells him, let me walk you through it. The Devil takes Bean back to when he was a teenager to his first act of crime. When you were just 15 years old, you had so much hatred in your heart towards your father for how he mistreated your mother and sister. Bean looks up with hatred in his eyes and says, he wasn't my father, he was a monster, and yes I hated him. The Devil laughs and speaks

Yes I know, and you want to know how I know because it was me who was speaking to you, putting the thought in your head to get revenge. So, the night you watched him leave the house, as he was walking down a dark alley, to come back home, you creeped up behind him and Boom!!!. Bean yells out, and he deserved it, for all the pain he caused for torching my mom and little sister. The devil agrees and says, oh yes, I'm sure he did but it was your first taste to kill, and after that you became obsessed, killing over and over again. The Devil showing Bean his victims. Bean begins crying out and lifts his head and sees a shadow of his mother saying, son pray. It's not too late. Mom, I'm sorry! Pray son, how I taught you. Suddenly Bean hears Joy talking. Baby! I don't know if you hear me, but you need to pray, call on Jehovah our God, and ask for forgiveness. Pray baby, even in your mind, God can hear you.

Let's pray. Joy begins praying over Bean. God who is our father, I come before you as a sinner broken and humble, Lord, I am asking for forgiveness of our sins and for all our transgression onto you, God, you said if we confess with our mouth and believe whole heartly that Jesus Christ, is your only and begotten son who died on the cross for our sins, that we will be saved and shall have everlasting life. Bean begins calling on God. God, I believe, I believe, please forgive me for all my sins and restore a new life within me. The Devil gets angry. Don't call that name down here, it's too late, you belong to me. Bean begins to pray harder. Jesus, I'm calling on you, to go to the father to intercede for me, please forgive me God for not believing in you. God, I believe in you.

Suddenly, Bean begins coughing, as he awakes, he sees Joy and becomes emotional crying out. Baby, I believe, I believe, God, is real. Joy begins crying and embracing him and she starts praising God saying. Thank you God, Thank You. As Bean comes back to realization he tries to speak and Joy tells him not now, just relax, be he insist to speak and is adamant to say something. He tells Joy I have to tell you the truth. Joy looking confused and asks Bean to tell me the truth about what? He looks at Joy with tears in his eyes and tells her they shot Flex. Joy becomes sympathetic and asks Bean is he dead. Bean looks and says he doesn't know. Joy gets hysterical and says we need to find out. Bean agrees and tells Joy, "I'm so sorry for everything, and this time I don't think I can fix it. Joy tells

Bean God will fix it. He then tells Joy, I'm the reason why Flex got shot. Joy asks Bean why?

Bean looks and says, because they want me, they want me. Joy looks fearful and asks, why do they want you Bean? Bean looks at Joy and tells her, it all started when I was 15 years old when I had my first taste of what it's like to kill. Joy's eyes widen as she becomes startled and asks Bean What are you talking about?" Bean tells Joy, if I'm going to give my life to God, I must confess my sins right? Joy tells him yes. Bean looks and tell Joy, I love you, but I have to tell you the truth. My stepdad didn't get rob, I was the one who killed him, it was me. Joy looks baffled, jumps up, and in a surprising tone says What! How could you do something like that? And as Joy looks at Bean with a stare of uncertainty he blots it out and tells her, I killed Jax. Joy instantly begins to scream and says no, no please tell me you're lying. "Omg! Who are you? Bean tries to calm Joy down by grabbing her arms pleading with her by saying, Baby, I'm sorry, I'm so sorry, please forgive me, please!. Joy starts crying and tells Bean, you lied to me, and I asked you over and over again and you lied to my face. You killed, Jax for what, for what Bean? He didn't deserve to die like that, you took him from his family and friends. And omg! You took your very own stepdad's life, and I don't want to hear about what he did, who gave you the right to decide if someone lives or dies? Joy tells Bean I can't do this with you anymore, I'm glad you found God, because you are going to need him to get through all of this, but it would have to be without me. Bean begins to beg and plead with Joy saying, Baby please don't leave me, I'll change, I promise, and I will show you everything you ever wanted from me, I promise I'll do it, but please just don't leave me. Joy grabs her belongings and turns to walk out the door. Then Bean begins screaming erratically, Joy, Joy please, don't go. Joy runs out of the door and Bean falls to his knees and calls on God asking him for forgiveness.

Live by the sword and you die by the sword.

Bean picks up the phone and calls his mom to check on her and tells her, hey mom, I just want to tell you I love you so much and I'm so sorry for everything I ever did to hurt you. Then Bean mom asks, son are you okay! Bean tells his mom, "I'm fine. I just wanted to call and tell you that and I'll see you soon. Bean mom replies, okay! Son, I love you too and see you soon. Bean gathers his belongings to check out the hotel room, and as he makes his way down the elevator he feels a sense of remorse for Flex and begins to tear up. He continues to exit the hotel making his way to his fancy car when he is approached by one of his crew members. Hey Bean, what's up? Bean looks and asks how did you know I was here? Oh! You know word get around then he asks, are you going to go see Flex, they say he is fighting hard for his life? Bean tells him yes and begin to tell him his experience he encountered saying, I'm putting all this behind me, I'm getting out of the game, and you should too. We don't have to live like this. Because God is real. Bean's crew member laughs and says, yea okay! I think you have been in that hotel room too long. Bean tells him no; I have been in the dark too long and now I see the light. Bean crew member asked him, so are you saying, You with God now. Bean looks at him and says, yes, and God is with me. Bean crew members walks away and then Bean asks, hey, did they find out who set Flex up? Bean crew member turns around and pulls out a gun and laughs and says, I did. It wasn't fun watching you make all the money and I get crumbs, so I did what I had to do, you understand how that goes right? Bean looks with tears in his eyes and his crew member tells him, no! don't cry, don't cry. You said you with God now right, Bean looks with tears running down his face and says, yes, and God is with me. Bean crew member aims the gun to his forehead and tells him. Well go to him then and fires two shot killing Bean instantly.

THE END.

Made in the USA
Middletown, DE
30 August 2024